To Baby Boy Shollenberger
From Great-Aunt Holly and Great-Uncle Scott

S0-AGU-473

ith great pride, I dedicate this book to the new branches on our ever-expanding family tree:

Callie Blake

Walker Blake

Macey Blake

Maggie Carrigan

Jackson Carrigan

Luke Carrigan

Emma Carrigan

Hannah Lucado

Preston Mota

Sylas Schliman Wallace

Riley Workman

Kaylin Workman

Kinley Workman

MAX LUCADO

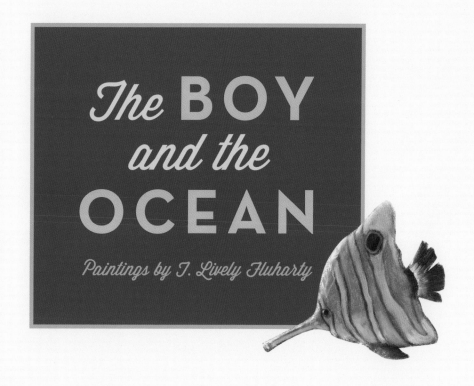

The **BOY**
and the
OCEAN

Paintings by T. Lively Fluharty

 **CROSSWAY**

WHEATON, ILLINOIS

 he little boy rolled over in his bed and opened his eyes. Through his window he could see the ocean.

Big and blue.
Rolling waves.
Water crashing on the beach.

The little boy stood at the window and searched for
the end of the ocean. He couldn't see it.

He could see the ships on it.
He could see the birds above it.
He could see the horizon stretched across it.
But the little boy couldn't see the end of it.
He couldn't see the end of the ocean.

"Would you like to play in the ocean?" his mother asked.

The little boy stood on the edge of the water with his mother.
She took his hand and they waded into the surf.

When the water covered his feet, he looked up at her.
When it reached his knees, he took a breath and
squeezed her hand.
When the wave rushed against his chest, she laughed.
He did, too.

The two sat in the sand and let the waves splash around them.
"God's love is like the ocean, my little boy," she said.

"It's always here.
It's always deep.
It never ends.
God's love is special."

The little boy spent the day playing near the ocean.
He counted starfish.
He built sandcastles.
He searched for shells.
But most of all—he watched the ocean.

He could see the clouds above it.
He could feel the tide within it.
He could taste the salt inside it.
But he could never see the end of it.
He could never see the end of the ocean.

That night, as the moonlight stretched across the sea
and landed on his face, he listened to the waves
slap, slap, slap against the sand.
"Go to sleep, my little boy," his mother whispered.
"The ocean will not leave. The ocean will not change.
The ocean is like God's love—

"Always here.
Always deep.
It never ends.
God's love is special."

And so the boy slept with the sound of the ocean in his ears.

The next day the little boy looked out a different
window at the mountains.

High and tall.
White-tipped.
Touching the clouds.

The little boy looked from side to side to see the end
of the mountains. He couldn't see it.

He could see the trees growing among them.
He could see the snow glistening on top of them.
He could see the birds flying around them.
But he couldn't see the end of the mountains.

"Would you like to hike the mountains?" his father asked.
He took the boy's hand and together they started up the
mountain trail.

When the leaves scattered over the boy's feet, he looked up at his father.
When the wind shook the tall trees, he took a breath and
squeezed his father's hand.
When they looked out over the great valley, the father smiled.
The boy did, too.

The two sat on a rock and looked around them.
"God's love is like the mountains, my little boy," the father said.

"It's always here.
It's always big.
It never ends.
God's love is special."

The two spent the day playing in the mountains.
The boy splashed in the creek.
He picked flowers in the meadow.
He listened to the singing birds.
But most of all—he looked at the mountains.

He could see the sky above them.
He could feel the wind blow through them.
He could hear the water that bubbled between them.
But he could never see the end of them.
He could never see the end of the mountains.

That night, as the moon appeared from behind the peaks, the boy thought of the mountains and smiled. "Go to sleep, my little boy," his father whispered. "The mountains will not leave. The mountains will not change. The mountains are like God's love—

"Always here.
Always tall.
It never ends.
God's love is special."

And so the boy slept with thoughts of mountains in his dreams.

The next day he ran on the beach and swam in the water.

He chased his puppy up the mountain trail and looked for flowers.

and looked at the night sky.

Stars everywhere!
Twinkling.
Shimmering.
Diamonds in the dark.

He looked as far as he could to see the end of the sky.
He couldn't see it.

He could see the moon, yellow and round.
He could see clouds, puffy and fat..
He saw a star race from one side of the sky to the other.
But he couldn't see the end of the sky.

"Would you like to count the stars?" his mother and father asked.
So they tried.

A dozen over there. Two dozen over there. There were too many!

When he reached a hundred, the boy
looked up at his mother.
When the wind turned chilly, his father
held him close.
His parents looked up into the big sky,
and became quiet.
So did he, for a while.

But then the boy spoke.
"God's love is like the night sky," he
told them.

"It's always here.
It's always big.
It never ends.
God's love is special."

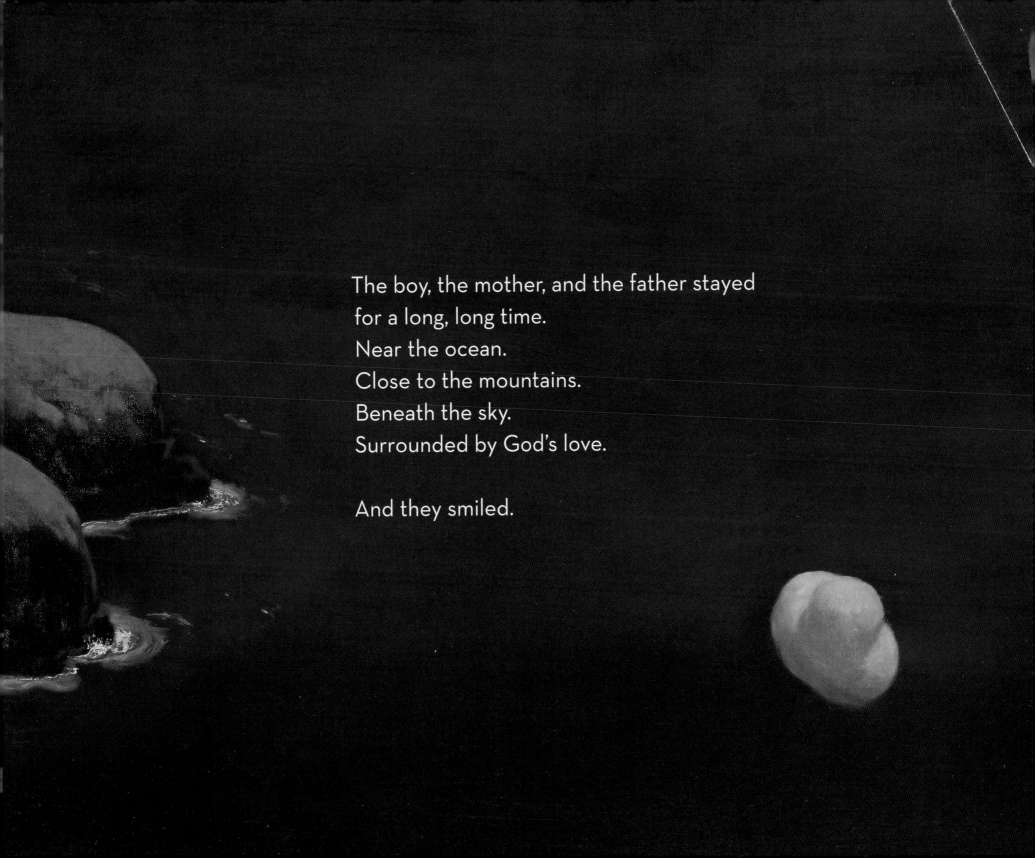

The boy, the mother, and the father stayed
for a long, long time.
Near the ocean.
Close to the mountains.
Beneath the sky.
Surrounded by God's love.

And they smiled.

The Boy and the Ocean

Text copyright © 2013 by Max Lucado

Illustrations copyright © 2013 by T. Lively Fluharty

Published by Crossway
   1300 Crescent Street
   Wheaton, Illinois 60187

All rights reserved. No part of this publication may be reproduced, stored in a retrieval system, or transmitted in any form by any means, electronic, mechanical, photocopy, recording, or otherwise, without the prior permission of the publisher, except as provided for by USA copyright law.

Cover design: Josh Dennis

Cover image: Illustrated by T. Lively Fluharty

First printing 2013

Printed in the United States of America

Hardcover ISBN: 978-1-4335-3931-2
PDF ISBN: 978-1-4335-3932-9
Mobipocket ISBN: 978-1-4335-3933-6
ePub ISBN: 978-1-4335-3934-3

Library of Congress Cataloging-in-Publication Data
Lucado, Max.
The boy and the ocean / Max Lucado ; illustrations by T. Lively Fluharty.
pages cm
Summary: "A boy learns about God's great, never-ending love from looking at the ocean, mountains, and sky"—Provided by publisher.
ISBN 978-1-4335-3931-2 (hc)
[1. God (Christianity)—Love—Fiction. 2. Chrisitan life—Fiction.] I.
Fluharty, T. Lively, illustrator. II. Title.
PZ7.L9684Bo 2013
[E]—dc23

       2012033800

Crossway is a publishing ministry of Good News Publishers.

LB 24 23 22 21 20 19 18 17 16 15 14 13
   15 14 13 12 11 10 9 8 7 6 5 4 3 2 1